To:_____
YP HIL
Hill, Susanna Leonard,
Grandma's girl :all the things I wish f

07/17/20

From:_____

With love for the special women I was lucky to have as grandmothers:
Muriel Bacheller Swatland and Gladys Lee Leonard.
—SLH

For my sweet Nona Bina and Ammi.
—LB

Published by Sourcebooks Wonderland, an imprint of Sourcebooks Kids
P.O. Box 4410, Naperville, Illinois 60567-4410
(630) 961-3900
sourcebookskids.com

Library of Congress Cataloging-in-Publication Data is on file with the publisher.

Source of Production: Wing King Tong Paper Products Co. Ltd., Shenzhen, Guangdong Province, China
Date of Production: December 2019
Run Number: 5016773

Printed and bound in China.
WKT 10 9 8 7 6 5 4 3 2 1

Grandma's Girl

All the Things I Wish for You!

WORDS BY *NEW YORK TIMES* BESTSELLING AUTHOR
SUSANNA LEONARD HILL

PICTURES BY LAURA BOBBIESI

sourcebooks
wonderland

Of all the most marvelous things in this world,
there are few that can truly compare
to the heartwarming, special, unbreakable bond
that a grandma and granddaughter share.

Dearest of granddaughters, heart of my heart,
there is something I want you to know.
You and I are alike in such wonderful ways
you will see more and more as you grow.

It probably seems like a long time ago,
but I was a girl just like you!
Curious, mischievous, lively, and bold,
always eager to try something new.

The world I grew up in was different, it's true,
and to you might seem funny or strange.

But inside, where it counts, we're alike, you and I.
What matters the most doesn't change.

I made snow angels, sand castles, mud pies, and forts,
swung as high as the swing let me fly!
Now we dance in the rain and make up silly games.
It's more fun with you there by my side.

Birthdays and playgrounds, best friends and games,
I knew all the same joys as you.

And if a bad dream woke me up in the night,
I snuggled up with *my* lovey too!

I wobbled uncertainly just as you did
whenever I tried something new.
But I practiced and practiced till I found my balance,
and one day, I know you will too.

I burned my first cake before learning to bake,
but then I got better with time.
My girl, keep on trying. Be fearless and proud!
You'll conquer each mountain you climb.

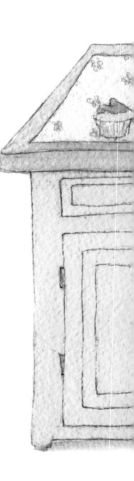

When faced with a challenge, be brave, take a chance.
Believe in yourself and jump in.

You might be surprised what you're capable of
when you let your daring side win.

You're clever and capable, smart as can be,
but should you have questions or doubt,

don't be shy about asking
for aid or advice.

You know I'm always there to help out.

It's important to speak out for what you believe.
Don't let anyone make you feel small.
So raise up your hand. Make sure you are heard.
Be your own unique you, and stand tall!

Show kindness to someone in need of a friend.
Be compassionate, giving, and good.

Most of all, be patient and kind to YOU too.
Love yourself every day as I would.

Truly, there is only one you in this world,

and you matter to friends,
family, and more.

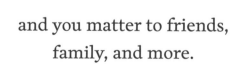

Remember to share your feelings and thoughts—
it's your true self who we all adore.

You have what it takes to get through the tough times.
Here's a secret I promise is true:
though it may not seem so, those hard times help you grow.
I got through them, and so you will too!

No matter if I am close by you or far,
you're always right here in my heart.
When you need me, I'll be there to listen and care.
There is nothing that keeps us apart.

You will change and you'll grow—and how far you will go—
in this wide open, wonder-filled world.
And I'll be here for you with a love deep and true,
because YOU are your grandma's best girl.

Dear _____

_____

_____

_____

_____

_____

_____

_____

_____

_____

With love, _____